NOW!

Tracey Corderoy

Tim Warnes

LITTLE TIGER PRESS
London

Archie found waiting
a little bit hard.

He wanted to have all the fun **NOW!**

Each day was full of exciting things.
And when did Archie want them . . . ?

But even Archie had to agree that **"NOW!"** wasn't always best . . .

Then one day Mum had exciting news.
They were going **on holiday!**

To help Archie wait they made a count-down chart. Dad used his special pens.

They played aeroplanes too . . .

and made a jumbo jet model.

As Archie crossed off the days, he got more and more excited . . .

Then finally it was time to go!

EXCEPT there was one
BIG problem . . .

"Wait!" cried Archie.

"We can't go
NOW!"

"I've lost Tiger!!"

They searched EVERYWHERE.

He MUST be here somewhere!

Why not take Elephant instead?

Mum and Dad checked the clock.
"We'll miss the plane!" they gasped.

Archie! We must go
NOW!!

They whisked Archie into the car.
And guess who
was there . . .

TIGER!

"Ahh, thank goodness!" said Mum. And off they went.

DEPARTURES

At the airport,
the queue was
ENORMOUS.

But Archie was
very, very patient.

Good boy!

Check-in

Please have your
tickets ready.

At last, they fastened their seatbelts.
And – **zoooom!**
– up went the plane.

"Was it worth the wait then, Archie?"
asked Dad.
But all Archie could say *now* was . . .